A Spot to Call Home
Written and Illustrated
by Kailyn Boyd

ISBN: 0578738147
ISBN-13: 978-0578738147

To Spot - thanks for being such a great dog!

My name is Spot which basically explains me.

I am a white dog with black spots. In early

fall, I was born in Georgia.

My mom, my four sisters,

and I would walk for a long time.

We would stop at creeks for water and beg for food. That worked up until spring. It had been two days since we had water. We were very thirsty and tired. A nice man gave us food and water. He put us in a fast truck that took us to a huge place with lots of barking friends! I was so scared.

They put me in this room with food, water, and a soft bed. I stayed there all alone for a couple days. Occasionally some little kids would play with me but I sadly would never see them again. I just wish that someone would want me to join their family and give me a forever home.

As I watched each family leave without me,
I wondered if it would be like this forever. A
new neighbor came, a big Golden Retriever that
would bark very loudly at all the little kids.

One day a nice looking family came to play with me. Unfortunately, it was thunder storming. I couldn't focus on playing with the two little girls because the noise frightened me.

I went to sit down in the mom's lap

because I was scared. She looked a little

surprised, but let me stay until I was

put back in my box.

I wondered if that was just going to be another group who would take home a different dog. But I felt that this family was different than the others. The two big people kept coming back to say hi, but the little kids couldn't because of my barking and jumping neighbor.

My favorite worker came and put me on a blue rope that guided me everywhere. Surprisingly, she gave the rope to the kind dad!

He carried me out the door and into the

thunderstorm. In the car, the two little

girls were waiting for me with big smiles.

After the family took me to their home, I wasn't scared anymore! I am happy that this will be my forever home and that I get to be with people who love me as much as I love them!

We adopted Spot.
Spot adopted us.

My family provided Spot food, shelter, love, and a home life that she deserved. We were surprised that Spot gave us much more love that we could ever give her. She eases pain, loneliness, anxiety, and keeps every one of us happy. She encourages us to exercise by walking with her. Dogs know how to comfort you and be your best friend when you need someone to love. Especially when they have gone through hard times, they know how to love a person and protect them.

Humane Societies encourage everyone to spay and neuter your pets to control the pet population and prevent homeless animals.

Kailyn Boyd wrote this book to help kids learn that getting pets from adoption centers saves lives. When we got Spot, she was a few days away from being put down because no one would take her home. We came, we saved a life, now it is your turn. Humane Societies have cats, dogs and many more pets, you can find your dream pet while saving a life at the same time.

About the Author and Illustrator,

Kailyn Boyd is a 7th grader in Atlanta. She lives with her parents and older sister. Kailyn is a Cadette Girl Scout and this book is part of her project to earn her Silver Award. She also speaks to young children about the importance of pet adoptions and pet care. She loves reading with her dog. Spot has made such a positive impact on her everyday life and she could not imagine having a more loving dog than her. Because of what Spot has done for her, she now greatly supports adoption centers because they truly help dogs and make a difference in not only the pets lives, but the people.

Made in the USA
Monee, IL
06 August 2020

37709374R00017